THE
JACKET I WEAR
IN THE SNOW

by **Shirley Neitzel**

pictures by

Nancy Winslow Parker

Greenwillow Books, New York

For Casey and P.W.
—S. N.

For Elaine and John
—N. W. P.

Watercolor paints, colored pencils,
and a black pen were used
for the full-color art.
The text type is Seagull.

The Jacket I Wear in the Snow
Text copyright © 1989
by Shirley Neitzel
Illustrations copyright © 1989
by Nancy Winslow Parker
Printed in Singapore
by Tien Wah Press
www.harperchildrens.com

First Edition
20 19 18 17 16 15 14 13 12 11

Library of Congress
Cataloging-in-Publication Data
Neitzel, Shirley.
The jacket I wear in the snow
by Shirley Neitzel;
pictures by Nancy Winslow Parker.
    p.   cm.
"Greenwillow Books."
Summary:
A young girl names all the
clothes that she must wear
to play in the snow.
ISBN 0-688-08028-6
ISBN 0-688-08030-8 (lib.bdg.)
ISBN 0-688-04587-1 (pbk.)
[1. Clothing and dress—Fiction.
2. Snow—Fiction.
3. Stories in rhyme.]
I. Parker, Nancy Winslow, ill.
II. Title.
PZ8.3.N34Jac   1989
[E]—dc19
88-18767   CIP   AC

This is the jacket I wear in the snow.

This is the zipper

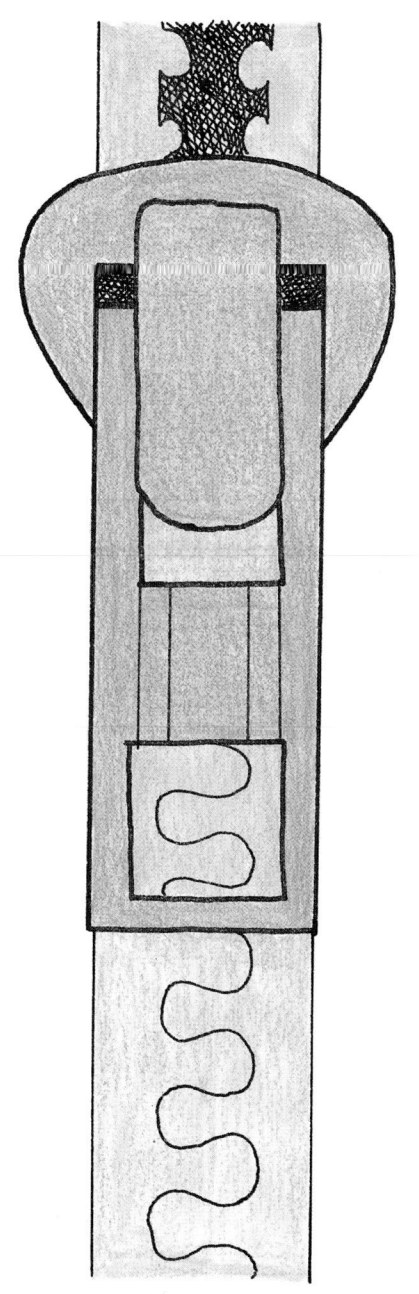

that's stuck on the  I wear in the snow.

This is the scarf, woolly and red,

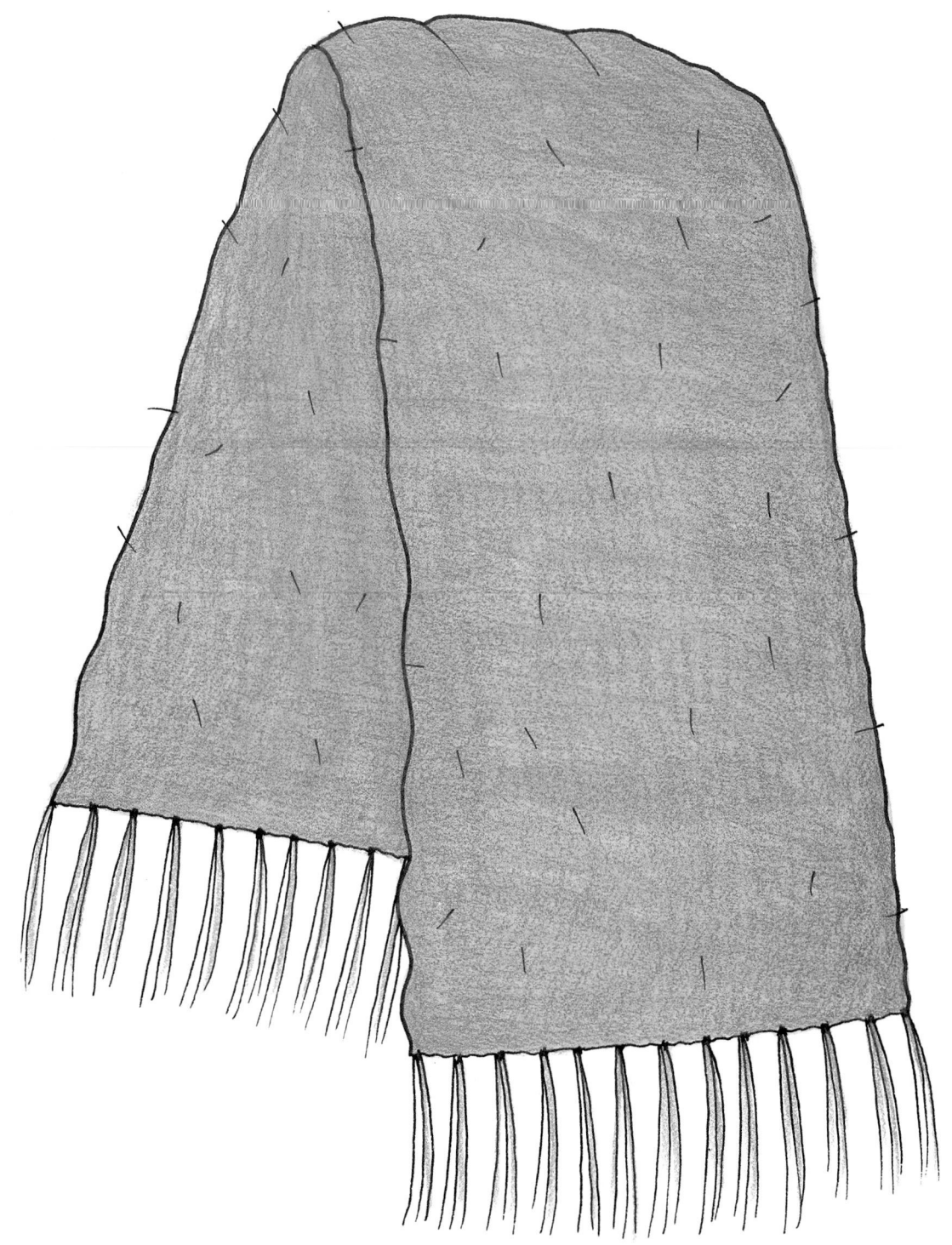

that's caught in the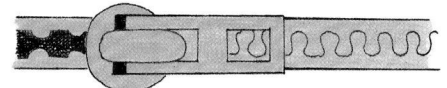

that's stuck on the  I wear in the snow.

This is the stocking cap for my head,

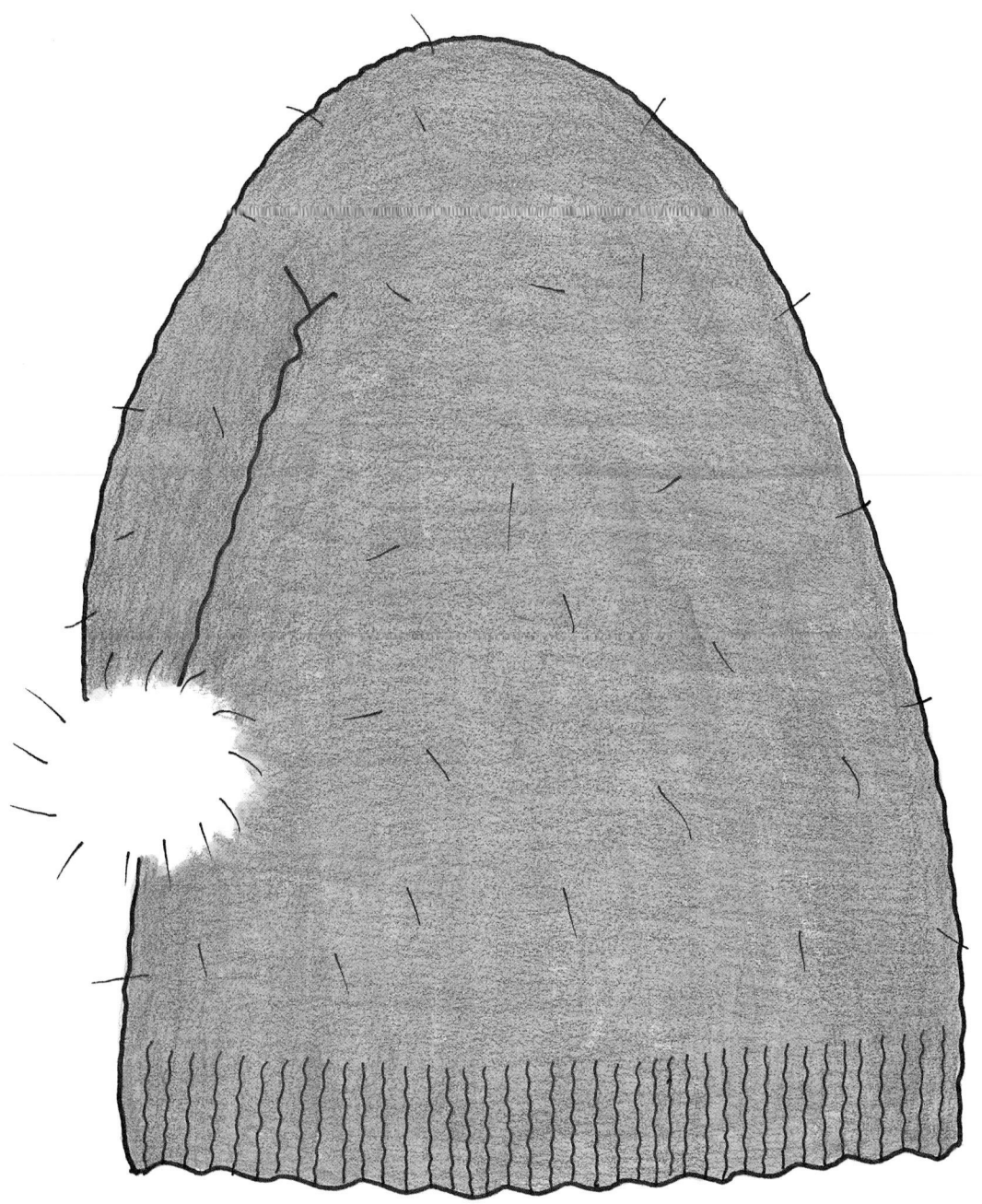

that matches the  woolly and red,

that's caught in the

that's stuck on the I wear in the snow.

These are the mittens that hang from each arm,

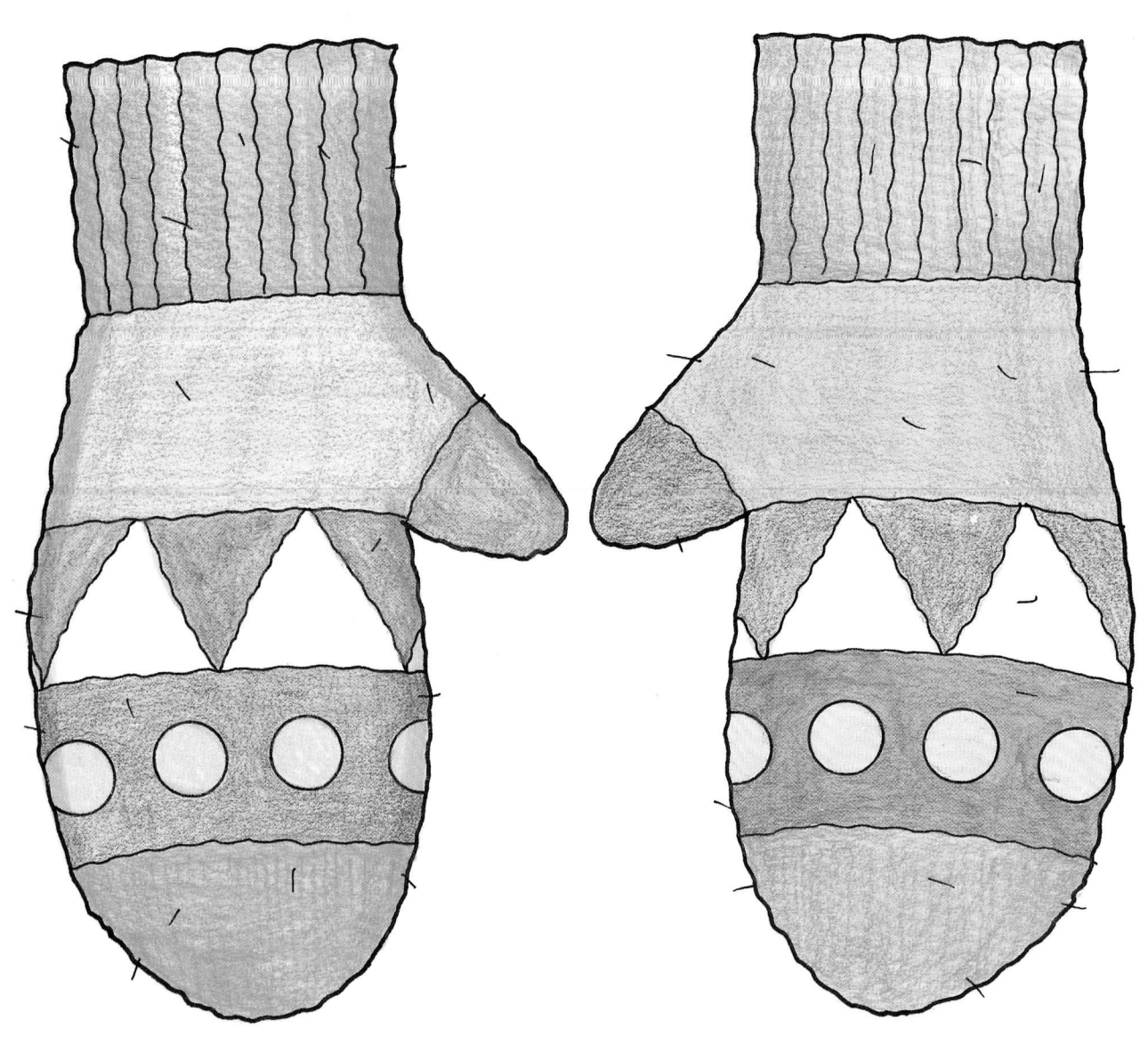

that I wear with the for my head,

that matches the woolly and red,

that's caught in the

that's stuck on the I wear in the snow.

This is the sweater all itchy and warm,

that meets the 🧤🧤 that hang from each arm,

that I wear with the 🧢 for my head,

that matches the 🧣 woolly and red,

that's caught in the 🔲 belt

that's stuck on the 🧥 I wear in the snow.

These are the jeans, stiff in the knee,

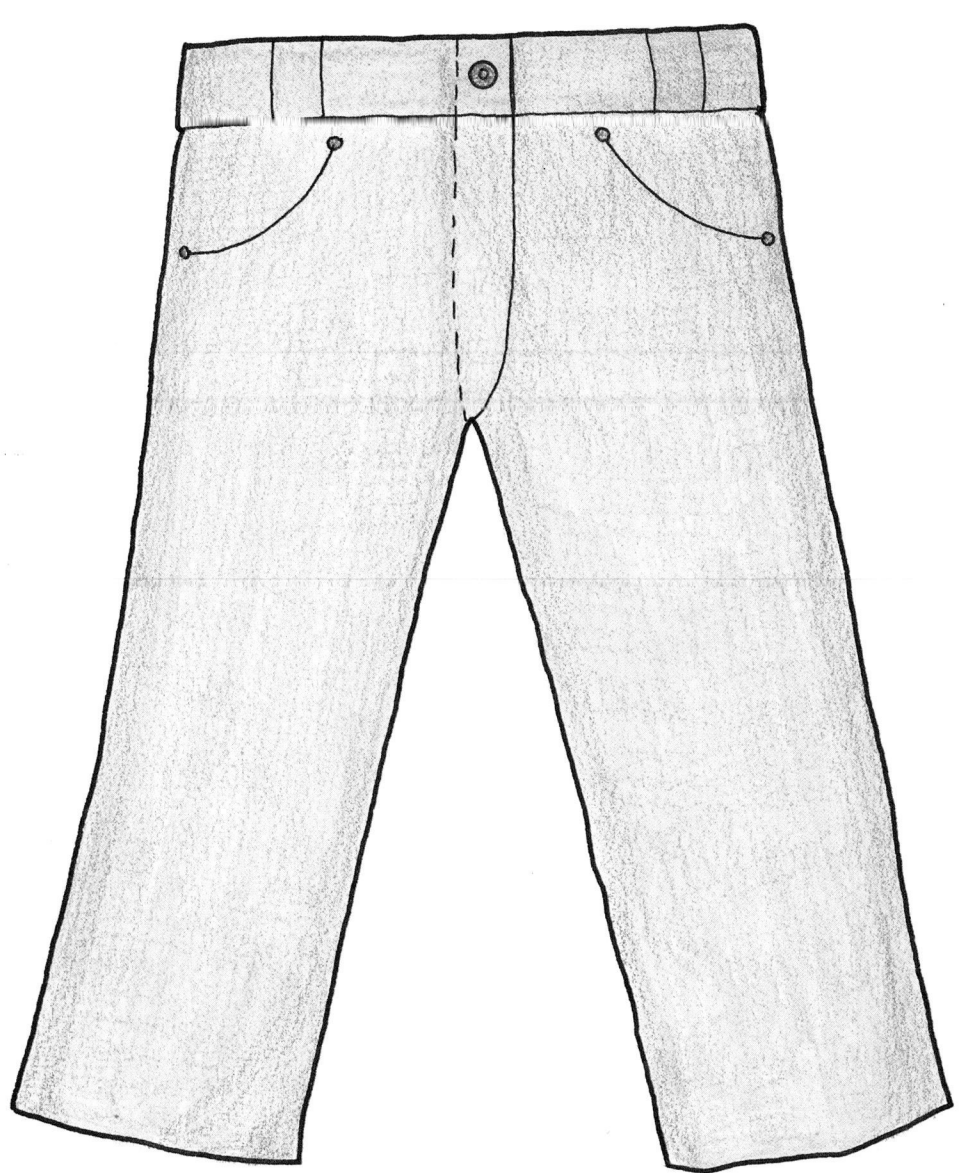

that go under the ⬚ all itchy and warm,

that meets the ⬚ that hang from each arm,

that I wear with the ⬚ for my head,

that matches the ⬚ woolly and red,

that's caught in the ⬚

that's stuck on the ⬚ I wear in the snow.

These are the boots, too big for me,

that cover the ![jeans] stiff in the knee,

that go under the ![sweater] all itchy and warm,

that meets the ![mittens] that hang from each arm,

that I wear with the ![hat] for my head,

that matches the ![scarf] woolly and red,

that's caught in the ![belt]

that's stuck on the ![coat] I wear in the snow.

This is long underwear, bunchy and hot,

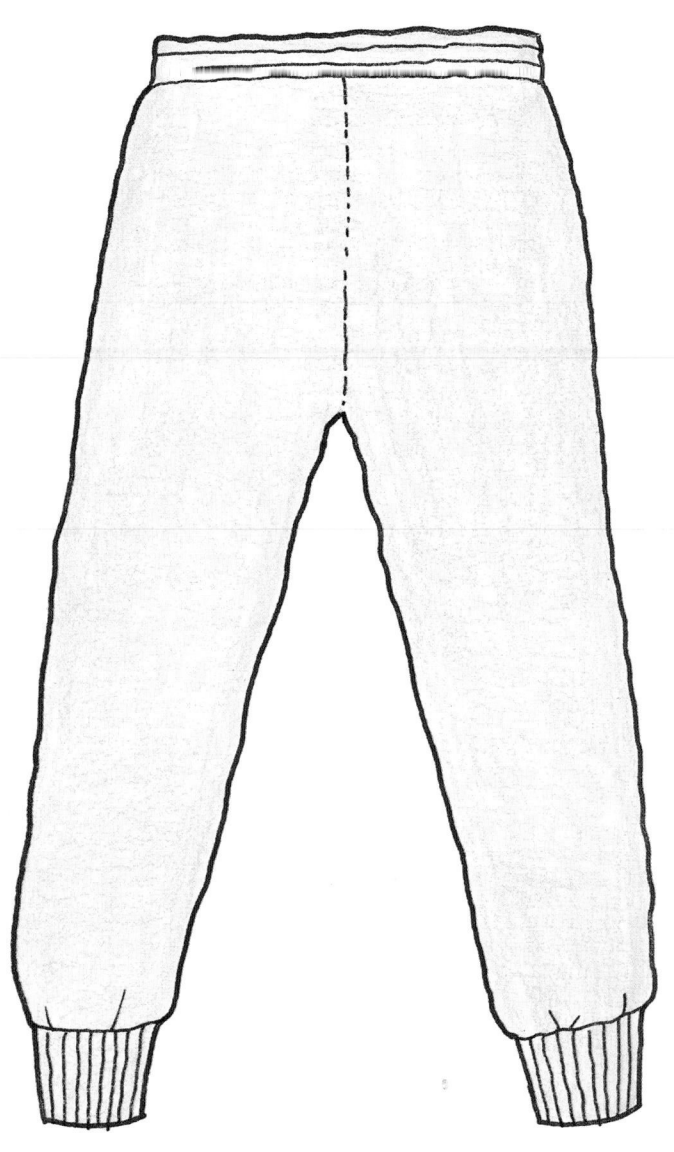

that is stuffed in the too big for me,

that cover the stiff in the knee,

that go under the all itchy and warm,

that meets the that hang from each arm,

that I wear with the for my head,

that matches the woolly and red,

that's caught in the

that's stuck on the I wear in the snow.

These are the socks, wrinkled a lot,

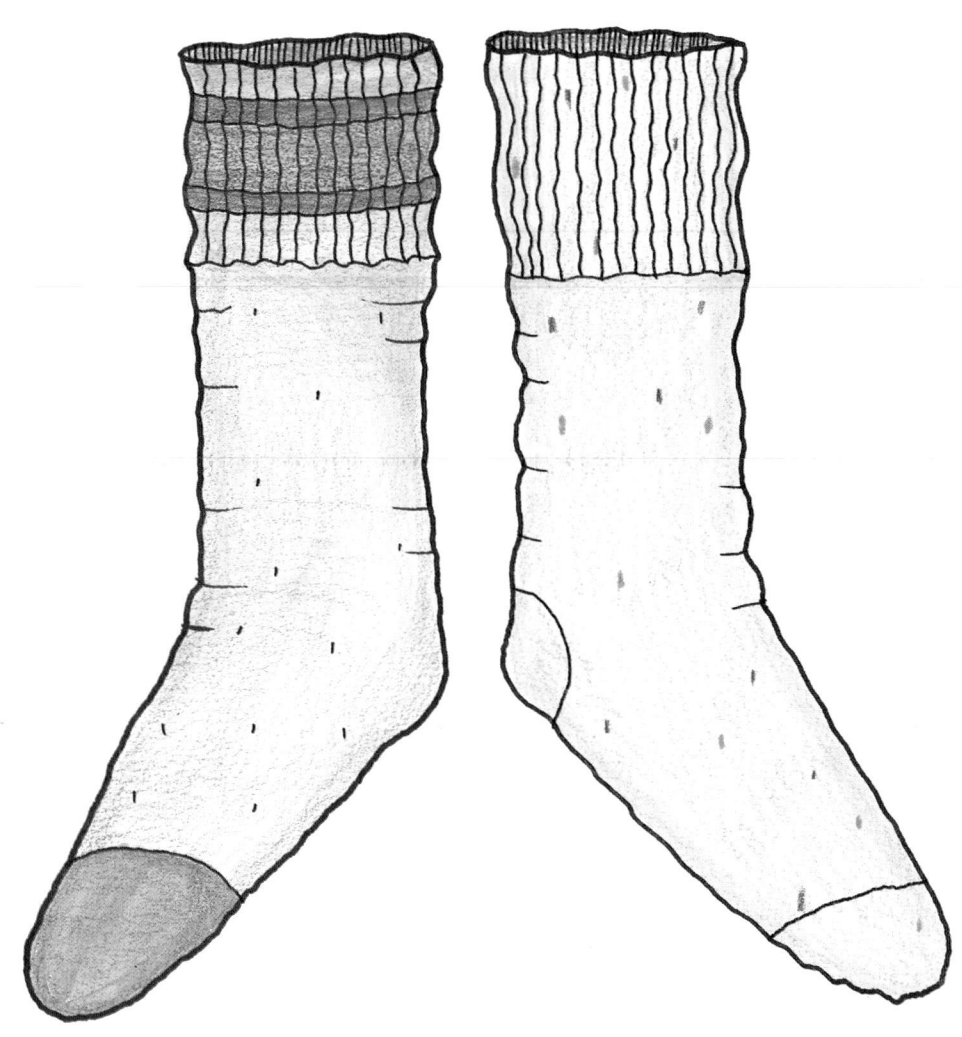

that are pulled over bunchy and hot,

that is stuffed in the too big for me,

that cover the stiff in the knee,

that go under the all itchy and warm,

that meets the that hang from each arm,

that I wear with the for my head,

that matches the woolly and red,

that's caught in the

that's stuck on the I wear in the snow.

These are the tears that fell from my eyes,

that dripped on the 🧦 wrinkled a lot,

that are pulled over 👖 bunchy and hot,

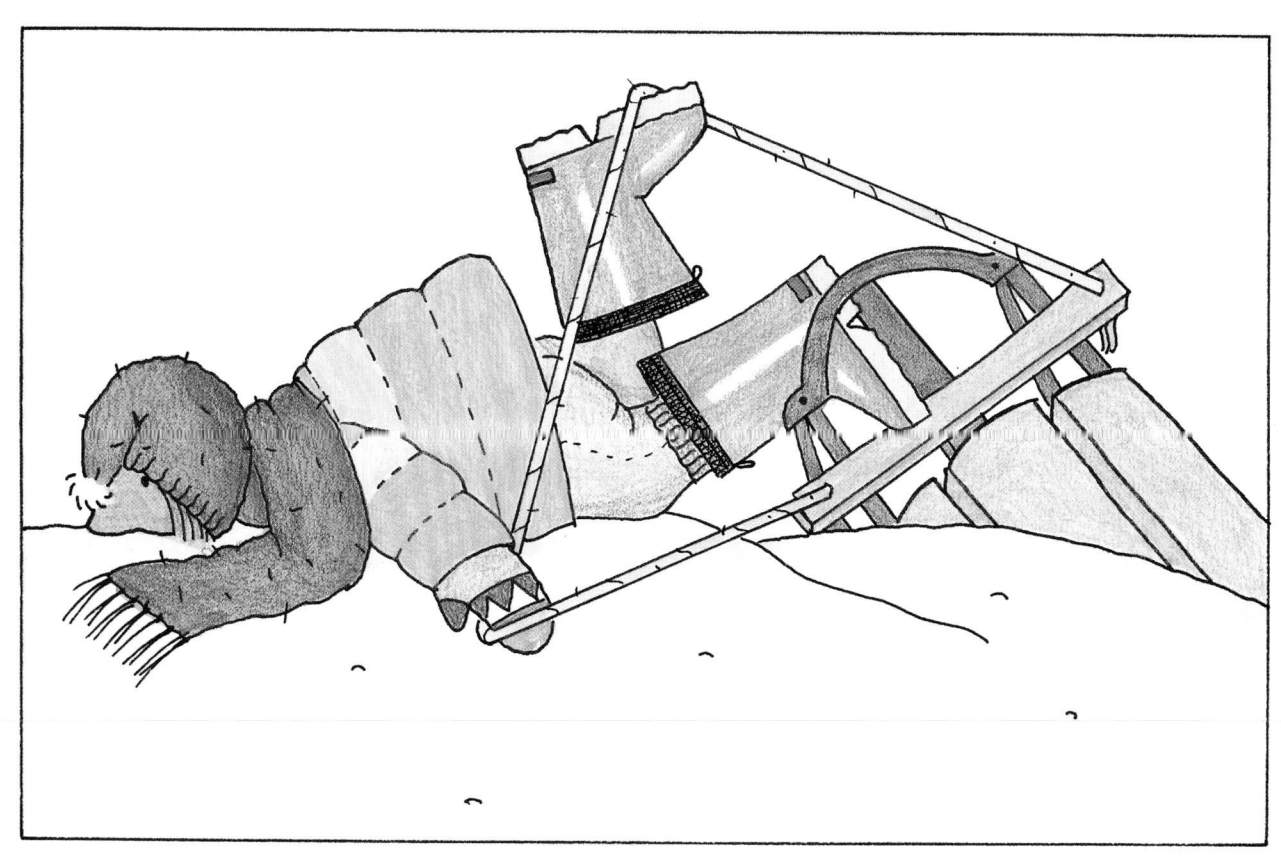

that is stuffed in the 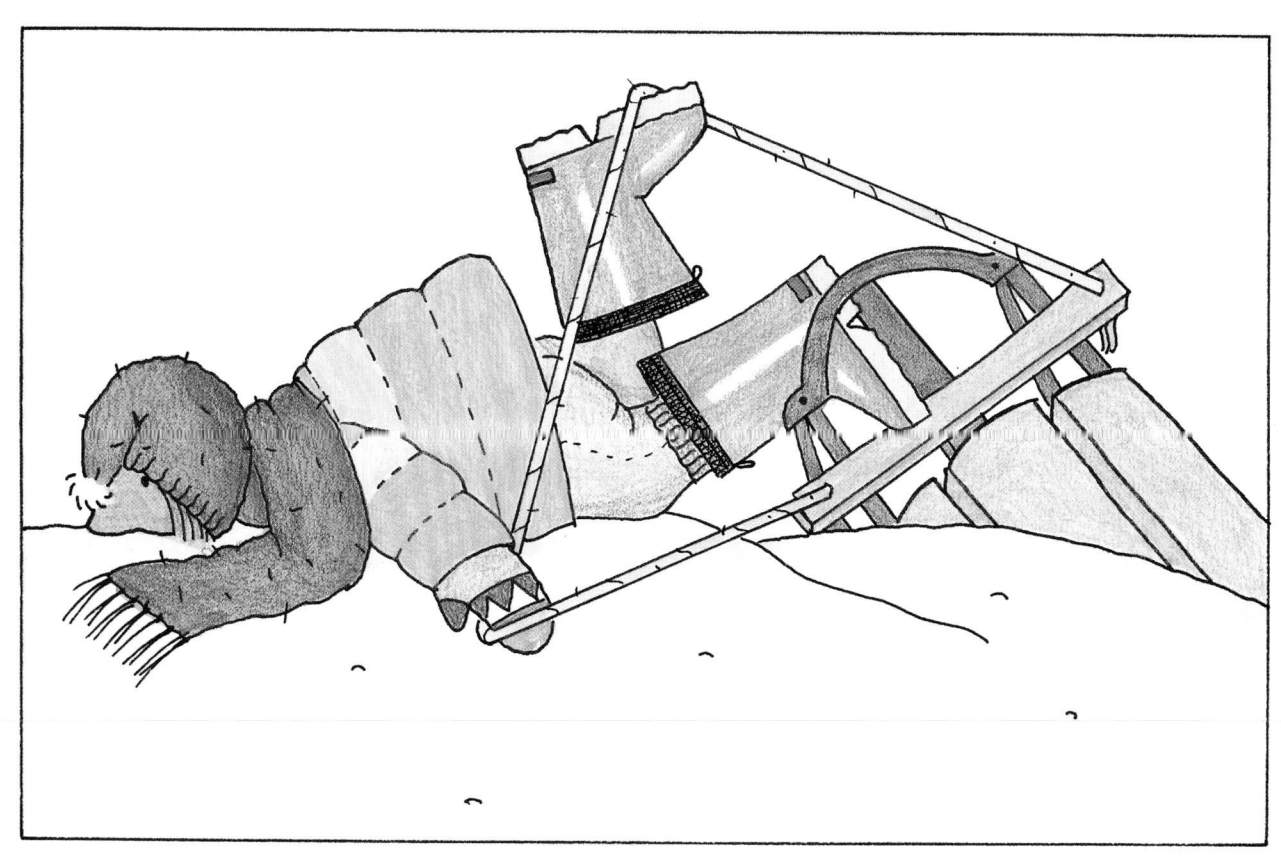 too big for me,

that cover the 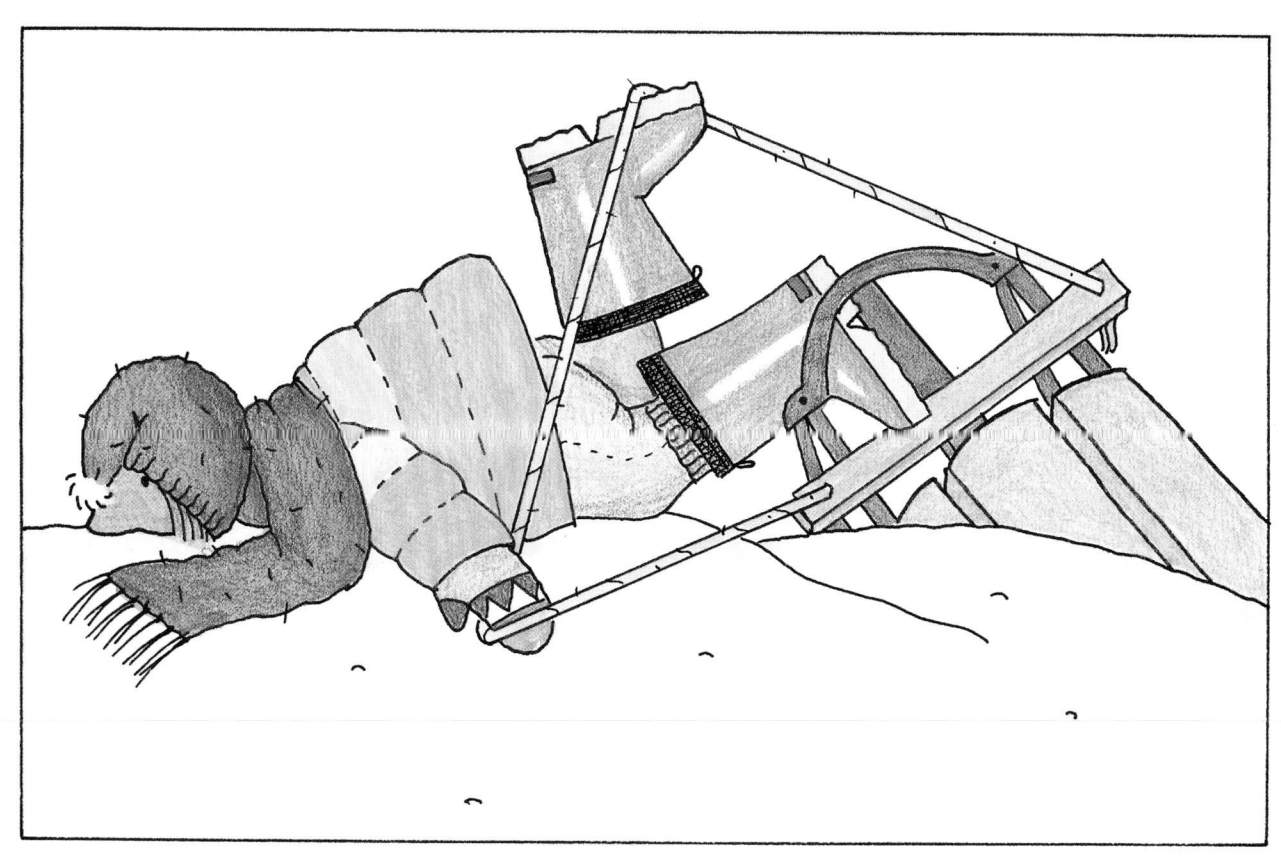 stiff in the knee,

that go under the 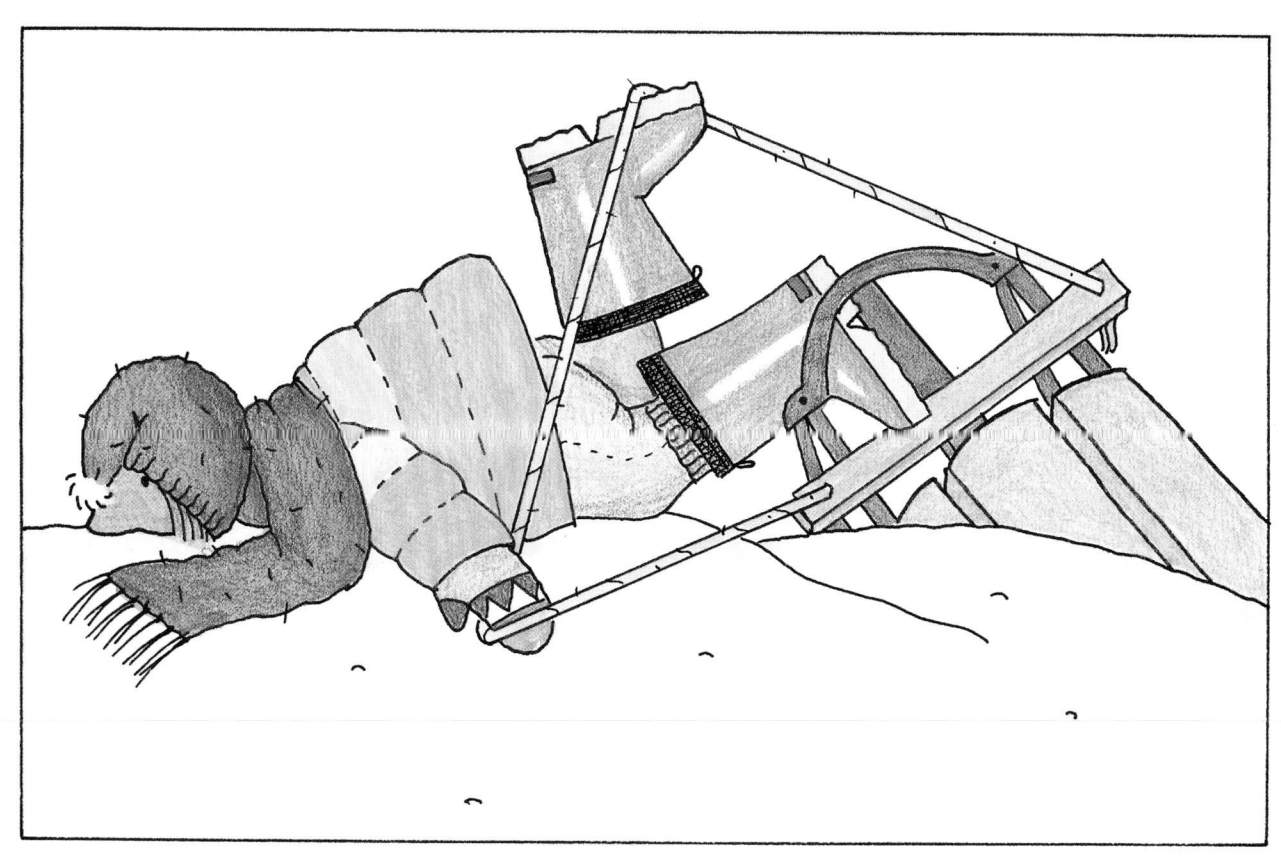 all itchy and warm,

that meets the 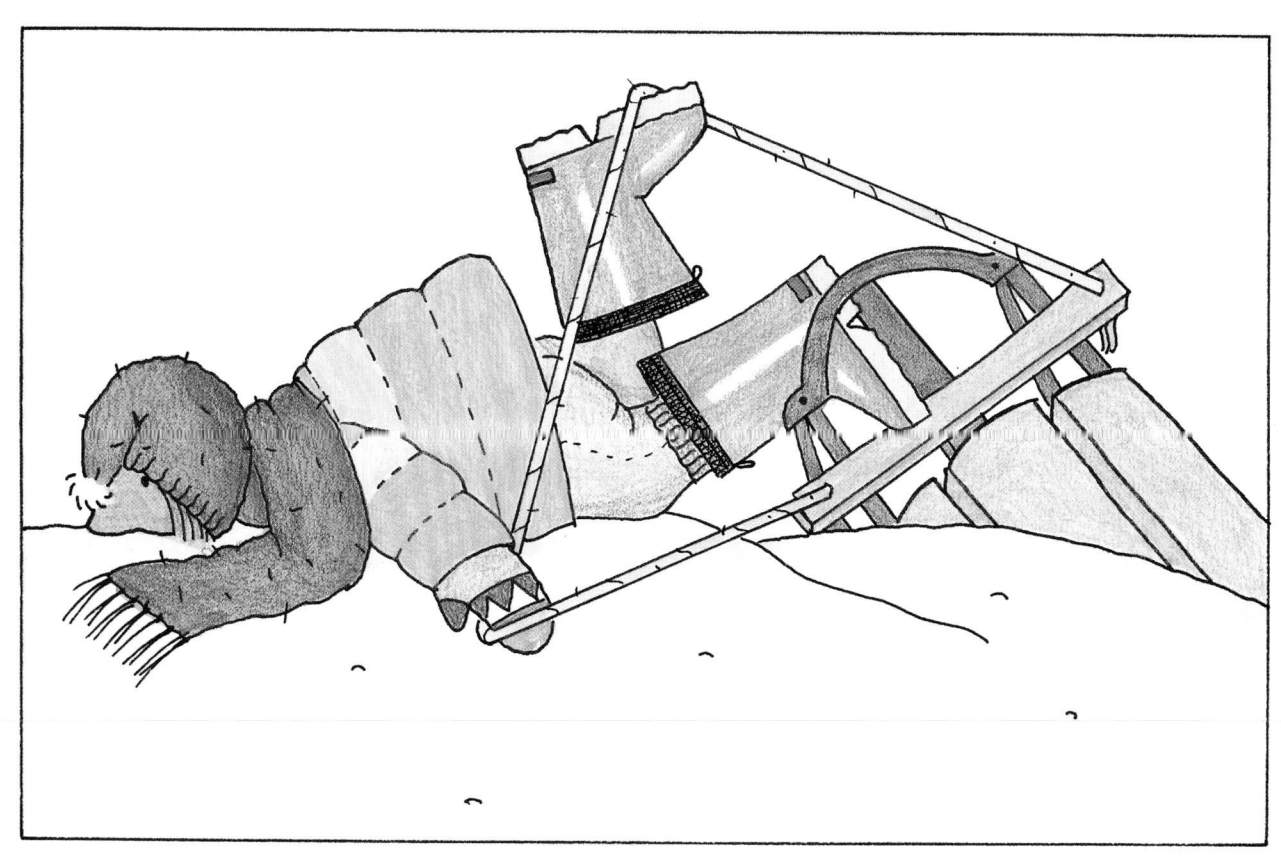 that hang from each arm,

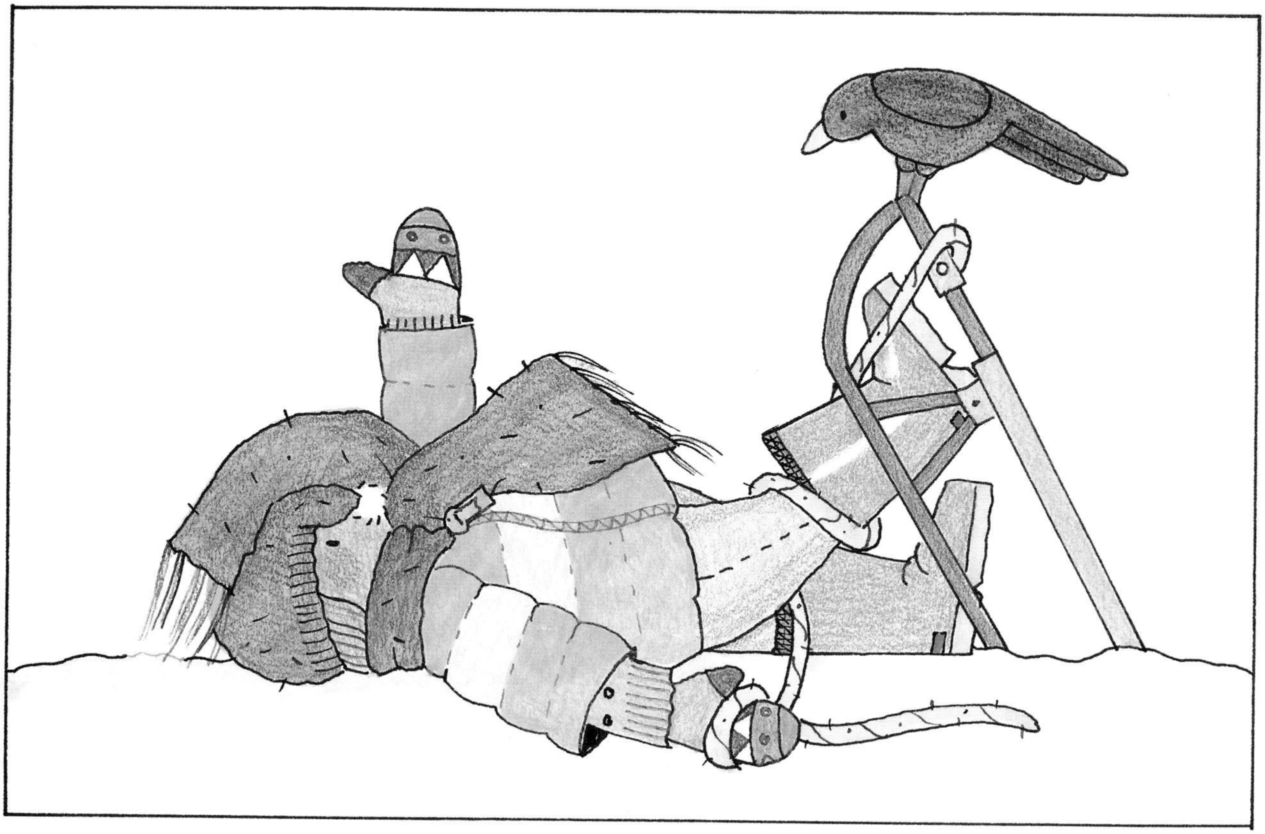

that I wear with the   for my head,

that matches the 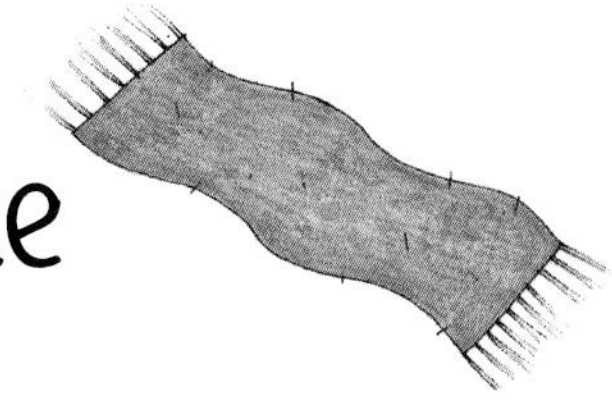 woolly and red,

that's caught in the

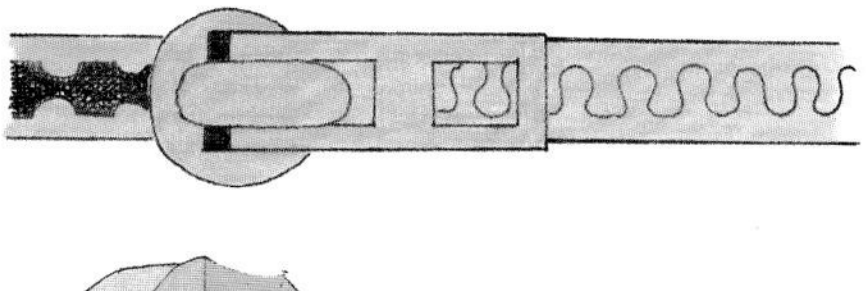

that's stuck on the I wear in the snow.

This is my mother, who heard my cries,
and wiped the tears that fell from my eyes,

and loosened the scarf, woolly and red,
and slipped off the stocking cap from my head,

and unpinned the mittens that hung from each arm,
and unbuttoned the sweater all itchy and warm,

and unzipped the boots, too big for me,
and straightened the jeans, stiff in the knee,

and smoothed the long underwear, bunchy and hot,

and pulled up the socks that were wrinkled a lot,

when she unstuck the zipper
of the jacket I wear in the snow.

jN P
Neitzel, Shirley.
The jacket I wear in the
snow

WITHDRAWN

Park Ridge Public Library

20 S. Prospect

Park Ridge, IL 60068

DEMCO

JAN   2004